Harry with Spots On

Chris Powling
and Scoular Anderson

First published in Great Britain by
A & C Black (Publishers) Ltd 1990
Published in Young Lions 1991
10 9 8 7 6 5

Young Lions is an imprint of the Children's Division,
part of HarperCollins Publishers Ltd,
77–85 Fulham Palace Road, London W6 8JB

Text copyright © Chris Powling 1990
Illustrations copyright © Scoular Anderson 1990

Printed and bound in Great Britain by
HarperCollins Manfacturing, Glasgow

Okay, I admit it. I was a teeny bit wild right from the start. Can you blame me, though?

There I sat in assembly, all goody-goodyish, and Mrs Cadett, our headteacher, suddenly told us that each class would be getting an end-of-term outing.

'End-of-term outings?' kids said.

So how come it was my WOW that
Mrs Cadett picked out?

'Harry!' she snapped. 'Settle *down*.
There's no need to get over-excited.'

Was it my fault that the kids all
around couldn't sit up properly?

If they weren't careful, Mrs Cadett would cancel these outings before our teachers had even organised them.

CHITTER
CHATTER

CHATTER

SHUSH!

SHUSH!

SHUSH!

This was when
our class teacher,
Miss Hobbs,
yanked me
outside into
the corridor
as if I'd been
mucking about.

She poked her nose so close to mine
that I went boss-eyed trying to look
at her. 'I was only helping, Miss,'
I said.

I ask you. Was that fair? No wonder
I went all moody.
'Harry?' said Miss Hobbs sharply.

Silly look? What silly look? My face was supposed to make her feel sorry for me. Trust a teacher to get it wrong.

Still, by the time assembly was over, I'd cheered up a lot. 'Our first job,' Miss Hobbs said to the class, 'is to choose where we want to go –

anywhere you like, so long as it doesn't take too long to get there. And providing all your mums and dads can afford it. Who's got some ideas?'

At once there was a hubbub.

Put us all to sleep, that would.

Museums are yawn-o.

Stately homes are better.

Yuk!

15

What do you say to Sea World?
GLUG-GLUG-GLUG-GLUG!
A funfair's the best place, I reckon.
yeah – to make yourself sick!

'SILENCE!' roared Miss Hobbs.

This is ridiculous. If you can't agree amongst yourselves I'll do the choosing.

'He's not *saying* anything, Miss,'
Samantha pointed out.

'You don't have to *listen*, Miss,'
Winston agreed.
'Just watch,' Sareeka added.

I was miming, you see.

Miss Hobbs frowned but let me get
on with it.
I acted out
a beach,

a zoo,

a museum,

a stately home,

a waxworks,

a bowling alley,

Sea World and a fun fair . . .

finishing off with the only place
that had them all:

The whole class clapped and
clapped and clapped.

Even Miss Hobbs was persuaded. 'Adventure Universe, Harry? I've heard it's a bit over-rated . . . but is that really where you want to go?'

And is it close enough for us to get there?

I wrote on the blackboard . . .

'Very funny,' said Miss Hobbs.

She couldn't tell us off, though,
because we'd done exactly what
she asked.

After that, I made sure I went on
doing exactly what she asked. I
mean, now I'd master-minded the
trip, I didn't want to be banned from
going on it.

And I made sure everyone else did
all the right things, too.

When Miss Hobbs told us we must
bring in letters of permission from
our parents,

I gave

everyone

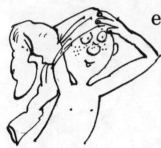

a reminder.

When she asked for the last of the
money to be brought in, I did the
collecting.

When she made
us practise
lining up
to be counted,

or walking in a
crocodile

or sitting sensibly
on the coach,

I drilled us till we were perfect.

All right, so maybe I was a bit wild again. Aren't kids allowed to be keen nowadays? In my opinion, they should have been grateful.

Miss Hobbs wasn't nearly as pleased as I'd expected.

Stop being such a fusspot, Harry.

A fusspot? Just because I sent her a checklist of all the things she had to sort out for the trip?

Checklist   tick here

letters to parents
Get coach
Send for brochures
Make worksheets if you want
tell everyone to bring coats in case its raining
extra hankies for nigel because he always forgets and he sniffs
Get bucket from caretaker for anyone who wants to be sick on the bus.
Tell everyone to   please turn over

Surely, putting a few ticks in a few boxes wasn't too much to ask? I felt really peeved, I can tell you.

But not as peeved as I felt just ten days before the outing . . .

I kept very quiet. To tell the truth,
I'd been wobbly inside since
Monday, but now wasn't the
moment to say so.

Already, Mum was having a good look at me. 'He's covered in spots,' she said.

What? Is it measles maybe?

'Just a few extra freckles, Mum,' I protested.

35

'It's not my fault, either,' I said
bitterly.
For once I was right.

But being right didn't make any difference. The next thing I knew, I was tucked up in bed with a thermometer under my tongue, waiting for the doctor.

'Measles,' said the doctor when she came. 'Don't worry, though. Now the spots are out, he'll start feeling better.'

'Ex-outing,' I said in a small voice.

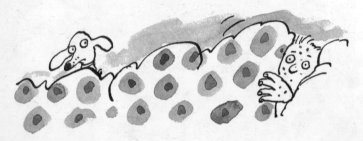

Then I hid my head under the pillow, in case anyone thought I was having a blub about it. Probably, that's why I didn't hear Mum and Dad whispering to each other. Really sneaky my mum and dad are.

That night, I dreamed about Adventure Universe. In my dream, I didn't have to go there because the whole place came to me. Don't ask me how. It just sprouted up all over our house.

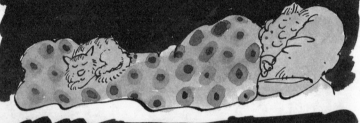

Once, when I woke up for a moment, I could've sworn I heard the actual bumping and scraping of the changeover being made, downstairs.

If only real life could be like that.
It isn't, though. Real life was a
Saturday morning with spots on –
and all my mates on a coach waving
at my house as they drove past on
the trip that *I'd* chosen. 'Bye!' I
called out spottily as I waved back.

I felt like a
burst balloon . . . .

BEEP!
BEEP!

Huh?

Was that another coach outside my
bedroom door?

BEEP!
BEEP!

It was! With my mum sitting in the
driving-seat!
'Hurry along, sir,' she called.
'We don't want to be late, do we?'

Mainly because I drove so nippily,
we got there on the stroke of opening
time. There wasn't even a queue,
as there usually is at these places.

We went to the beach first.

Then we went to the zoo.

The museum was next.

After that, a visit to a stately home . . .

And then the waxworks . . .

And the bowling alley . . .

Sea World cropped up just before lunch.

Only the funfair could finish off a
trip like this.

Going home was as much fun as the outward journey.

It had certainly been a day to remember. To tell the truth, I was even ready to put my feet up and have a bit of a rest.

I think that my sneaky, lovely
mum and dad were, too.

KNOCK KNOCK!

Who was it at the door? Was that
Miss Hobbs I could hear? She
sounded really fed up.

'I'm so sorry to trouble you,' she said. 'But the coach has broken down outside your gate, and goodness knows when we'll get back to school! Some of the kids are bursting to go to the loo, I'm afraid. They told me Harry's mum and dad wouldn't mind a bit if . . .'

'That would be the last straw.' Miss
Hobbs shuddered. 'What a terrible
day it's been . . .'

The kids began trooping in to use the toilet. They looked pretty miserable, but what they saw when they opened the toilet door seemed to cheer them up.

That's when I had my stroke of
genius. It was the sort of idea you
get only once in your life. (Well,
maybe a few times more, in my case.)

Hopping with excitement, I leant
over the bannister and called,
'Mum? Dad? Can you come up here
a minute? I've just had a brainwave.'

Probably you've guessed what the
brainwave was.

Mum and Dad agreed straight away. We'd treat the whole class to the Adventure Harryverse experience! Naturally, I gave myself a starring role. Well, if you'd thought it up, wouldn't you have gone really wild?

When the class had been round
everything, Miss Hobbs was so
pleased that I think she'd have
given me a hug – spots and all –
if I hadn't been out of reach.

Harry, your adventure park is terrific. It knocks spots off the real thing!

'Three cheers for Harry!' someone shouted.

The whole street must have echoed with hip-hip hoorays, as the mended coach took my mates back to school to be met by their parents.

Next day, I had about a million get-well cards. And a couple of big kids from the secondary school came knocking on our door to see if Adventure Harryverse was still open. 'How much do you charge?' they asked.

Best of all, though, was Mrs Cadett's assembly, when I got back.

By then, everyone knew the story
but she still told it again.

We won't bother with
an outing next year. We'll
get Harry's mum and dad
to turn the whole school into
an adventure park!

Won't it be W I L D ?

Especially since all the kids have
promised to come with spots painted
on their faces.